Are You Kitten Me?

A Hiss-terical Book of Cat Puns

by Fitz the Cat and friends

Right meow, you're probably wondering what you've gotten yourself into.

This book isn't the
tail of a cat,

but a cat-alogue of cat puns.

Purrhaps you'll agree that they're funny...

...or maybe you'll find them to be a cat-astrophe,

or even a

claw-amity.

But let's stay paw-sitive!

This book is purr-ty short,

so you know there
isn't a meow-ntain
of groans to be had.

But, purr-sonally,

we think you'll
feline-d them to be
mew-sic to your
ears.

At the very mew-nimum, this book will whisker you away

with some claw-ful puns.

Isn't that what makes it so purr-fect?

Don't furr-get it in the hiss-tory of books you once decided to read!

Beg our paw-don
for making you
read such
a-paw-lling lines.

But hopefully these puns have you feline fine!

If you've pounced on your own copy, make sure you keep it fur-ever...

...if only so you can pick it up and ask yourself again,

"Are you kitten me?"

THE END

60452574R00017

Made in the USA
Middletown, DE
15 August 2019